THE PETER YARROW SONGBOOK

Let's Sing Together!

ILLUSTRATED BY

Terry Widener

STERLING

New York / London

I dedicate all the recordings for *Let's Sing Together!* to Pete Seeger,
the one who led me, taught me, and inspired me, along with his compatriots in The Weavers,
on the path I've gratefully taken as a singer and an activist. —P. Y.

To my children, and my wife, Leslie, who sang songs together,
and to my French agent, Michèle. —T. M. W.

STERLING and the distinctive Sterling logo are registered trademarks of Sterling Publishing Co., Inc.

Library of Congress Cataloging-in-Publication Data Available

2 4 6 8 10 9 7 5 3 1

Published by Sterling Publishing Co., Inc.
387 Park Avenue South, New York, NY 10016
All songs are traditional with new lyrics and music by Peter Yarrow and Bethany Yarrow © 2009
Silver Dawn Music, ASCAP
Additional text © 2009 by Peter Yarrow
Illustrations © 2009 by Terry Widener
Distributed in Canada by Sterling Publishing
c/o Canadian Manda Group, 165 Dufferin Street
Toronto, Ontario, Canada M6K 3H6
Distributed in the United Kingdom by GMC Distribution Services Castle Place,
166 High Street, Lewes, East Sussex, England BN7 1XU
Distributed in Australia by Capricorn Link (Australia) Pty. Ltd.
P.O. Box 704, Windsor, NSW 2756, Australia

Printed in China
All rights reserved

Sterling ISBN 978-1-4027-5963-5

For information about custom editions, special sales,
premium and corporate purchases, please contact
Sterling Special Sales Department at 800-805-5489
or specialsales@sterlingpublishing.com.

The artwork for this book was created using acrylic paints.

CONTENTS

INTRODUCTION
PETER YARROW

When I had just turned sixteen, I became a junior counselor at Sprout Lake Camp for Cardiac Kids, where we all had a deep commitment to giving campers from the poorest communities in New York City all the joy and happiness possible, knowing they might have only this one summer left. When we sang together, magically, a great sense of closeness emerged, as fear, teasing, and concern about the children's illnesses melted away.

Years later, with the indescribable sense of history being made, these same songs lifted me and my partners in Peter, Paul, & Mary to unforgettable heights at the 1963 March on Washington for Civil Rights as hope became concrete and fear of what we faced melted away.

In small but no less meaningful ways, they lifted my wife, our young children, and me when we sang together as we drove cross-country in "Big Red." At Peter, Paul, & Mary concerts, in our homes, and in ways that taught caring and respect in my children's classrooms, these songs reasserted their remarkable magic.

These songs were, for me, the sound track of the most meaningful parts of my life.
Through this book and CD, I wish some of the same for you.

This Little Light of Mine

This little light of mine,
I'm gonna let it shine.
This little light of mine,
I'm gonna let it shine.
This little light of mine,
I'm gonna let it shine,
Let it shine, let it shine, let it shine.

Everywhere I go,
I'm gonna let it shine.
Everywhere I go,
I'm gonna let it shine.
Everywhere I go,
I'm gonna let it shine,
Let it shine, let it shine, let it shine.

In my brother's heart,
I'm gonna let it shine.
In my brother's heart,
I'm gonna let it shine.
In my brother's heart,
I'm gonna let it shine,
Let it shine, let it shine, let it shine.

In my sister's soul,
I'm gonna let it shine.
In my sister's soul,
I'm gonna let it shine.
In my sister's soul,
I'm gonna let it shine,
Let it shine, let it shine, let it shine.

All around the world,
I'm gonna let it shine.
All around the world,
I'm gonna let it shine.
All around the world,
I'm gonna let it shine,
Let it shine, let it shine, let it shine.

This little light of mine,
I'm gonna let it shine.
This little light of mine,
I'm gonna to let it shine.
This little light of mine,
I'm gonna let it shine,
Let it shine, let it shine, let it shine.

She'll Be Coming 'Round the Mountain

She'll be coming 'round the mountain when she comes.
She'll be coming 'round the mountain when she comes.
She'll be coming 'round the mountain,
She'll be coming 'round the mountain,
She'll be coming 'round the mountain when she comes.

She'll be driving six white horses when she comes.
She'll be driving six white horses when she comes.
She'll be driving six white horses,
She'll be driving six white horses,
She'll be driving six white horses when she comes.

We will get the old red rooster when she comes.
We will get the old red rooster when she comes.
We will get the old red rooster,
We will get the old red rooster,
We will get the old red rooster when she comes.

And we'll all have chicken and dumplings when she comes.
And we'll all have chicken and dumplings when she comes.
And we'll all have chicken and dumplings,
And we'll all have chicken and dumplings,
And we'll all have chicken and dumplings when she comes.

She'll be wearing red pajamas when she comes.
She'll be wearing red pajamas when she comes.
She'll be wearing red pajamas,
She'll be wearing red pajamas,
She'll be wearing red pajamas when she comes.

She'll be coming 'round the mountain when she comes.
She'll be coming 'round the mountain when she comes.
She'll be coming 'round the mountain,
She'll be coming 'round the mountain,
She'll be coming 'round the mountain when she comes.

Hey, Lolly, Lolly

Hey, lolly, lolly, lolly,
Hey, lolly, lolly low.
Hey, lolly, lolly, lolly,
Hey, lolly, lolly low.

Make up verses as you go along,
Hey, lolly, lolly low.
That's the way we sing this song,
Hey, lolly, lolly low.

Hey, lolly, lolly, lolly,
Hey, lolly, lolly low.
Hey, lolly, lolly, lolly,
Hey, lolly, lolly low.

Well, I got a gal, ten feet tall,
Hey, lolly, lolly low.
Sleeps in the kitchen with her feet in the hall,
Hey, lolly, lolly low.

Hey, lolly, lolly, lolly,
Hey, lolly, lolly low.
Hey, lolly, lolly, lolly,
Hey, lolly, lolly low.

I got a gal, three feet tall,
Hey, lolly, lolly low.
Sleeps in the kitchen with her feet in the kitchen,
Hey, lolly, lolly low.

Hey, lolly, lolly, lolly,
Hey, lolly, lolly low.
Hey, lolly, lolly, lolly,
Hey, lolly, lolly low.

Foolish verses suit me fine,
Hey, lolly, lolly low.
They don't even have to rhyme (at all),
Hey, lolly, lolly low.

Hey, lolly, lolly, lolly,
Hey, lolly, lolly low.
Hey, lolly, lolly, lolly,
Hey, lolly, lolly low.

Glad you're here to be my friend,
Hey, lolly, lolly low.
That's the way my days should end,
Hey, lolly, lolly low.

Hey, lolly, lolly, lolly,
Hey, lolly, lolly low.
Hey, lolly, lolly, lolly,
Hey, lolly, lolly low.

Home on the Range

Oh, give me a home where the buffalo roam,
And the deer and the antelope play,
Where seldom is heard a discouraging word
And the skies are not cloudy all day.

Home, home on the range,
Where the deer and the antelope play,
Where seldom is heard a discouraging word
And the skies are not cloudy all day.

Where the water's so pure and the breeze is so free,
And the air is so balmy and light,
I would not exchange my fine home on the range
For all of your cities so bright.

Home, home on the range,
Where the deer and the antelope play,
Where seldom is heard a discouraging word
And the skies are not cloudy all day.

How often at night where the heavens are so bright
With the light from the glittering stars,
Have I stood there amazed, and asked as I gazed,
If their glory exceeds that of ours.

Home, home on the range,
Where the deer and the antelope play,
Where seldom is heard a discouraging word
And the skies are not cloudy all day.

Oh, give me a land where the bright diamond sand
Glows its light from the glittering streams,
Where glideth the graceful and beautiful swan,
Like the maid in my heavenly dreams.

Home, home on the range,
Where the deer and the antelope play,
Where seldom is heard a discouraging word
And the skies are not cloudy all day.

Blue-Tail Fly

When I was young I used to wait
On master and give him his plate,
And pass the bottle when he got dry,
And brush away the blue-tail fly.

Jimmie crack corn and I don't care,
Jimmie crack corn and I don't care,
Jimmie crack corn and I don't care,
My master's gone away.

And when he'd ride around the farm,
The flies so numerous, they did swarm.
One chanced to bite him on the thigh,
The devil take the blue-tail fly!

Jimmie crack corn and I don't care,
Jimmie crack corn and I don't care,
Jimmie crack corn and I don't care,
My master's gone away.

The pony run, he jump, he pitch,
He threw my master in the ditch.
He died and the jury wondered why.
The verdict was the blue-tail fly.

Jimmie crack corn and I don't care,
Jimmie crack corn and I don't care,
Jimmie crack corn and I don't care,
My master's gone away.

They laid him under a 'simmon tree.
His epitaph is there to see.
Beneath that stone he's forced to lie—
A victim of the blue-tail fly.

Jimmie crack corn and I don't care,
Jimmie crack corn and I don't care,
Jimmie crack corn and I don't care,
My master's gone away.

Hey, Ho, Nobody Home

Hey, ho, nobody home,
Meat, nor drink, nor money have I none.
Yet shall we be merry.

Hey, ho, nobody home,
Meat, nor drink, nor money have I none.
Yet shall we be merry.

Hey, ho, nobody home,
Meat, nor drink, nor money have I none.
Yet shall we be merry.

Hey, ho, nobody home.

My Bonnie Lies over the Ocean

My Bonnie lies over the ocean,
My Bonnie lies over the sea,
My Bonnie lies over the ocean,
Oh, bring back my Bonnie to me.

Bring back, oh, bring back,
Oh, bring back my Bonnie to me, to me.
Bring back, oh, bring back,
Oh, bring back my Bonnie to me.

My Bonnie is calling me gently,
My Bonnie is calling me home,
My Bonnie is calling me sweetly,
I feel so sad and alone.

Bring back, oh, bring back,
Oh, bring back my Bonnie to me, to me.
Bring back, oh, bring back,
Oh, bring back my Bonnie to me.

Last night as I lay on my pillow,
Last night as I lay in my sleep,
Last night as I lay on my pillow,
I felt my sad eyes start to weep.

Bring back, oh, bring back,
Oh, bring back my Bonnie to me, to me.
Bring back, oh, bring back,
Oh, bring back my Bonnie to me.

Oh, blow ye winds over the ocean,
Oh, blow ye winds over the sea,
Oh, blow ye winds over the ocean,
And bring back my Bonnie to me.

Bring back, oh, bring back,
Oh, bring back my Bonnie to me, to me.
Bring back, oh, bring back,
Oh, bring back my Bonnie to me.

I'm on My Way

I'm on my way
And I won't turn back.
And I'm on my way
And I won't turn back.
I'm on my way
And I won't turn back.
I'm on my way, great God,
I'm on my way.

And I asked my father,
"Won't you go with me?"
And I asked my father,
"Won't you go with me?"
I asked my father,
"Won't you go with me?"
I'm on my way, great God,
I'm on my way.

And if he say no,
I'll go anyhow.
And if he say no,
I'll go anyhow.
And if he say no,
I'll go anyhow.
I'm on my way, great God,
I'm on my way.

And I asked my mother,
"Won't you go with me?"
And I asked my mother,
"Won't you go with me?"
And I asked my mother,
"Won't you go with me?"
I'm on my way, great God,
I'm on my way.

I'm on my way
And I won't turn back.
I'm on my way
And I won't turn back.
I'm on my way
And I won't turn back.
I'm on my way, great God,
I'm on my way.

And if she say no,
I'll go anyhow.
And if she say no,
I'll go anyhow.
And if she say no,
I'll go anyhow.
I'm on my way, great God,
I'm on my way.

And I'm on my way
To the freedom land.
And I'm on my way
To the freedom land.
And I'm on my way
To the freedom land.
I'm on my way, great God,
I'm on my way.

We Shall Not Be Moved

We shall not,
We shall not be moved.
We shall not,
We shall not be moved.
Just like a tree that's standing by the water,
We shall not be moved.

Young and old together,
We shall not be moved.
Young and old together,
We shall not be moved.
Just like a tree that's standing by the water,
We shall not be moved.

We shall not,
We shall not be moved.
We shall not,
We shall not be moved.
Just like a tree that's standing by the water,
We shall not be moved.

Black and white together,
We shall not be moved.
Black and white together,
We shall not be moved.
Just like a tree that's standing by the water,
We shall not be moved.

We shall not,
We shall not be moved.
We shall not,
We shall not be moved.
Just like a tree that's standing by the water,
We shall not be moved.

We're marching for our children,
We shall not be moved.
We're marching for our parents,
We shall not be moved.
Just like a tree that's standing by the water,
We shall not be moved.

We shall not,
We shall not be moved.
We shall not,
We shall not be moved.
Just like a tree that's standing by the water,
We shall not be moved.

Down by the Riverside

I'm gonna lay down my sword and shield
Down by the riverside,
Down by the riverside,
Down by the riverside.
I'm gonna lay down my sword and shield
Down by the riverside.
Study war no more.

I ain't gonna study war no more,
I ain't gonna study war no more,
I ain't gonna study war no more.
I ain't gonna study war no more,
I ain't gonna study war no more,
I ain't gonna study war no more.

I'm gonna walk with that Prince of Peace
Down by the riverside,
Down by the riverside,
Down by the riverside.
I'm gonna walk with that Prince of Peace
Down by the riverside.
Study war no more.

I ain't gonna study war no more,
I ain't gonna study war no more,
I ain't gonna study war no more.
I ain't gonna study war no more,
I ain't gonna study war no more,
I ain't gonna study war no more.

I'm gonna lay down that atom bomb
Down by the riverside,
Down by the riverside,
Down by the riverside.
I'm gonna lay down that atom bomb
Down by the riverside.
Study war no more.

I ain't gonna study war no more,
I ain't gonna study war no more,
I ain't gonna study war no more.
I ain't gonna study war no more,
I ain't gonna study war no more,
I ain't gonna study war no more.

I'm gonna shake hands around the world
Down by the riverside,
Down by the riverside,
Down by the riverside.
I'm gonna shake hands around the world
Down by the riverside.
Study war no more.

I ain't gonna study war no more,
I ain't gonna study war no more,
I ain't gonna study war no more.
I ain't gonna study war no more,
I ain't gonna study war no more,
I ain't gonna study war no more.

Oh, You Can't Get to Heaven

Oh, you can't get to heaven on roller skates,
'Cause you'll roll right by those pearly gates.
Oh, you can't get to heaven on roller skates,
'Cause you'll roll right by those pearly gates.
I ain't gonna grieve my Lord no more.

I ain't gonna grieve my Lord no more,
I ain't gonna grieve my Lord no more,
I ain't gonna grieve my Lord no more.

Oh, you can't get to heaven on a rocking chair,
'Cause rocking out won't get you there.
Oh, you can't get to heaven on a rocking chair,
'Cause rocking out won't get you there.
I ain't gonna grieve my Lord no more.

I ain't gonna grieve my Lord no more,
I ain't gonna grieve my Lord no more,
I ain't gonna grieve my Lord no more.
I ain't gonna grieve my Lord no more,
I ain't gonna grieve my Lord no more,
I ain't gonna grieve my Lord no more.

Oh, you can't get to heaven on a rocket ship,
'Cause the Lord don't think that a rocket ship's hip.
Oh, you can't get to heaven on a rocket ship,
'Cause the Lord don't think that ship is hip.
I ain't gonna grieve my Lord no more.

I ain't gonna grieve my Lord no more,
I ain't gonna grieve my Lord no more,
I ain't gonna grieve my Lord no more.
I ain't gonna grieve my Lord no more,
I ain't gonna grieve my Lord no more,
I ain't gonna grieve my Lord no more.

Oh, you can't get to heaven on fossil fuel,
'Cause the Lord's gone green 'cause he knows it's cool.
Oh, you can't get to heaven on fossil fuel,
'Cause the Lord's gone green—he knows it's cool.
I ain't gonna grieve my Lord no more.

I ain't gonna grieve my Lord no more,
I ain't gonna grieve my Lord no more,
I ain't gonna grieve my Lord no more.
I ain't gonna grieve my Lord no more,
I ain't gonna grieve my Lord no more,
I ain't gonna grieve my Lord no more.

NOTES TO MY FELLOW "PICKERS"

A s you review the lyrics to the songs printed on the following pages, you will see the chord names (with diagrams showing you where to put your fingers on the strings) above the words indicating where each new chord begins.

Finally, please don't feel you have to stick with the chords I'm playing at all. I'm always changing and developing my accompaniments—sometimes I change back to earlier chord patterns, then return again. In folk music, making these changes is not only allowed, it's expected and admired as part of a music that celebrates the gifts of each individual to interpret the music as he or she sees fit. Making changes to a folk song is called "the folk process," which means that new players change the song's lyrics, melody, rhythmic feel, and accompaniment to suit themselves and make the songs feel right and relevant in their own times.

Have fun creating your own folk process.
The songs will appreciate it and feel loved, I promise you.

This Little Light of Mine

C

This little light of mine,

C 7

I'm gonna let it shine.

F

This little light of mine,

C

I'm gonna let it shine.

C

This little light of mine,

E 7   A m

I'm gonna let it shine,

C   G   F   C
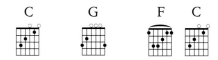

Let it shine, let it shine, let it shine.

Everywhere I go,
I'm gonna let it shine.
Everywhere I go,
I'm gonna let it shine.
Everywhere I go,
I'm gonna let it shine,
Let it shine, let it shine, let it shine.

In my brother's heart,
I'm gonna let it shine.
In my brother's heart,
I'm gonna let it shine.
In my brother's heart,
I'm gonna let it shine,
Let it shine, let it shine, let it shine.

In my sister's soul,
I'm gonna let it shine.
In my sister's soul,
I'm gonna let it shine.
In my sister's soul,
I'm gonna let it shine,
Let it shine, let it shine, let it shine.

All around the world,
I'm gonna let it shine.
All around the world,
I'm gonna let it shine.
All around the world,
I'm gonna let it shine,
Let it shine, let it shine, let it shine.

This little light of mine,
I'm gonna let it shine.
This little light of mine,
I'm gonna to let it shine.
This little light of mine,
I'm gonna let it shine,
Let it shine, let it shine, let it shine.

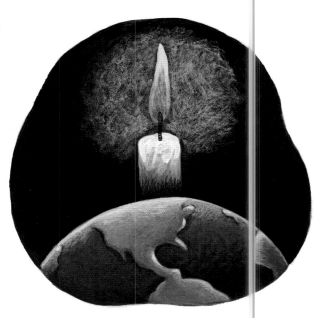

She'll Be Coming 'Round the Mountain

D

She'll be coming 'round the mountain when she comes.

A

She'll be coming 'round the mountain when she comes.

D　　　　**D 7**

She'll be coming 'round the mountain,

G

She'll be coming 'round the mountain,

D　　　**A**　　　**D**

She'll be coming 'round the mountain when she comes.

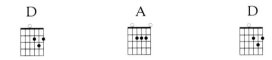

She'll be driving six white horses when she comes.
She'll be driving six white horses when she comes.
She'll be driving six white horses,
She'll be driving six white horses,
She'll be driving six white horses when she comes.

We will get the old red rooster when she comes.
We will get the old red rooster when she comes.
We will get the old red rooster,
We will get the old red rooster,
We will get the old red rooster when she comes.

And we'll all have chicken and dumplings when she comes.
And we'll all have chicken and dumplings when she comes.
And we'll all have chicken and dumplings,
And we'll all have chicken and dumplings,
And we'll all have chicken and dumplings when she comes.

She'll be wearing red pajamas when she comes.
She'll be wearing red pajamas when she comes.
She'll be wearing red pajamas,
She'll be wearing red pajamas,
She'll be wearing red pajamas when she comes.

She'll be coming 'round the mountain when she comes.
She'll be coming 'round the mountain when she comes.
She'll be coming 'round the mountain,
She'll be coming 'round the mountain,
She'll be coming 'round the mountain when she comes.

Hey, Lolly, Lolly

Chorus:

C

Hey, lolly, lolly, lolly,

G

Hey, lolly, lolly low.

G

Hey, lolly, lolly, lolly,

C

Hey, lolly, lolly low.

Make up verses as you go along,
Hey, lolly, lolly low.
That's the way we sing this song,
Hey, lolly, lolly low.

Chorus

Well, I got a gal, ten feet tall,
Hey, lolly, lolly low.
Sleeps in the kitchen with her feet in the hall,
Hey, lolly, lolly low.

Chorus

I got a gal, three feet tall,
Hey, lolly, lolly low.
Sleeps in the kitchen with her feet in the kitchen,
Hey, lolly, lolly low.

Chorus

Foolish verses suit me fine,
Hey, lolly, lolly low.
They don't even have to rhyme (at all),
Hey, lolly, lolly low.

Chorus

Glad you're here to be my friend,
Hey, lolly, lolly low.
That's the way my days should end,
Hey, lolly, lolly low.

Chorus

Home on the Range

If you place your capo on the 2nd fret and play in the key of D major, this song will sound in the same key as on the CD: E major.

D (E)   G (A)

Oh, give me a home where the buffalo roam,

D (E)   E 7 (F#7) A 7 (B 7)

And the deer and the antelope   play,

D (E)   D 7 (E 7) G (A)

Where seldom is heard a discouraging word

D (E)   A (B)   D (E)

And the skies are not cloudy all day.

D (E) A 7 (B 7)   D (E)

Home, home   on the range,

E 7(F#7)   A 7 (B 7)

Where the deer and the antelope play,

D (E)   D 7 (E 7) G (A)   E m 7(F#m 7)

Where seldom is heard a discouraging word

D (E)   A (B)   D (E)

And the skies are not cloudy all day.

Where the water's so pure and the breeze is so free,
And the air is so balmy and light,
I would not exchange my fine home on the range
For all of your cities so bright.

Home, home on the range,
Where the deer and the antelope play,
Where seldom is heard a discouraging word
And the skies are not cloudy all day.

How often at night where the heavens are so bright
With the light from the glittering stars,
Have I stood there amazed, and asked as I gazed,
If their glory exceeds that of ours.

Home, home on the range,
Where the deer and the antelope play,
Where seldom is heard a discouraging word
And the skies are not cloudy all day.

Oh, give me a land where the bright diamond sand
Glows its light from the glittering streams,
Where glideth the graceful and beautiful swan,
Like the maid in my heavenly dreams.

Home, home on the range,
Where the deer and the antelope play,
Where seldom is heard a
discouraging word
And the skies are not cloudy
all day.

Blue-Tail Fly

E A

When I was young I used to wait

E B 7

On master and give him his plate,

A

And pass the bottle when he got dry,

B E

And brush away the blue-tail fly.

Chorus:

E B 7

Jimmie crack corn and I don't care,

E

Jimmie crack corn and I don't care,

E 7 A

Jimmie crack corn and I don't care,

E B 7 E

My master's gone away.

And when he'd ride around the farm,
The flies so numerous, they did swarm.
One chanced to bite him on the thigh,
The devil take the blue-tail fly!

Chorus

The pony run, he jump, he pitch,
He threw my master in the ditch.
He died and the jury wondered why.
The verdict was the blue-tail fly.

Chorus

They laid him under a 'simmon tree.
His epitaph is there to see.
Beneath that stone he's forced to lie—
A victim of the blue-tail fly.

Chorus

Hey, Ho, Nobody Home

Em D C Em

Hey, ho, nobody home,

Em   D   C   Em

Meat, nor drink, nor money have I none.

Em   D   C Em

Yet shall we be mer- ry.

Hey, ho, nobody home,
Meat, nor drink, nor money have I none.
Yet shall we be merry.

Hey, ho, nobody home,
Meat, nor drink, nor money have I none.
Yet shall we be merry.

Hey, ho, nobody home.

My Bonnie Lies over the Ocean

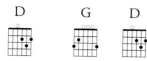

My Bonnie lies over the ocean,

My Bonnie lies over the sea,

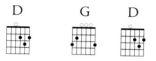

My Bonnie lies over the ocean,

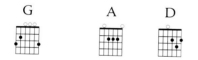

Oh, bring back my Bonnie to me.

Chorus:

Bring back, oh, bring back,

Oh, bring back my Bonnie to me, to me.

Bring back, oh, bring back,

Oh, bring back my Bonnie to me.

My Bonnie is calling me gently,
My Bonnie is calling me home,
My Bonnie is calling me sweetly,
I feel so sad and alone.

Chorus

Last night as I lay on my pillow,
Last night as I lay in my sleep,
Last night as I lay on my pillow,
I felt my sad eyes start to weep.

Chorus

Oh, blow ye winds over the ocean,
Oh, blow ye winds over the sea,
Oh, blow ye winds over the ocean,
And bring back my Bonnie to me.

Chorus

John Jacob Jingleheimer Schmidt

D   A

John Jacob Jingleheimer Schmidt,

D

His name is my name too.

D 7   G

Whenever we go out, we hear the happy people shout,

A   D

"There goes John Jacob Jingleheimer Schmidt!"

A

La la la la la la la!

I'm on My Way

D

I'm on my way

A

And I won't turn back.

A

And I'm on my way

D

And I won't turn back.

D 7

I'm on my way

G

And I won't turn back.

D   A

I'm on my way, great God,

D

I'm on my way.

And I asked my father,
"Won't you go with me?"
And I asked my father,
"Won't you go with me?"
I asked my father,
"Won't you go with me?"
I'm on my way, great God,
I'm on my way.

And if he say no,
I'll go anyhow.
And if he say no,
I'll go anyhow.
And if he say no,
I'll go anyhow.
I'm on my way, great God,
I'm on my way.

And I asked my mother,
"Won't you go with me?"
And I asked my mother,
"Won't you go with me?"
And I asked my mother,
"Won't you go with me?"
I'm on my way, great God,
I'm on my way.

And if she say no,
I'll go anyhow.
And if she say no,
I'll go anyhow.
And if she say no,
I'll go anyhow.
I'm on my way, great God,
I'm on my way.

And I'm on my way
To the freedom land.
And I'm on my way
To the freedom land.
And I'm on my way
To the freedom land.
I'm on my way, great God,
I'm on my way.

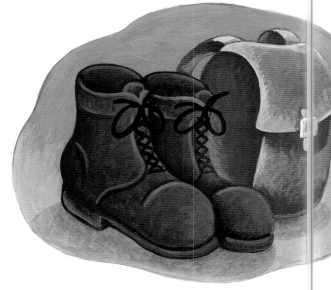

We Shall Not Be Moved

If you place your capo on the first fret and play in the key of E major, this song will sound in the same key as on the CD: F major.

Chorus:

E (F)

We shall not,

B 7 (C 7)

We shall not be moved.

B 7 (C 7)

We shall not,

E (F)

We shall not be moved.

E 7 (F 7)   A (Bb)   E (F)

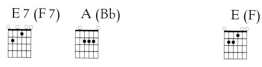

Just like   a tree that's standing by the water,

B 7 (C 7)   E (F)

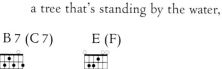

We shall not   be   moved.

Young and old together,
We shall not be moved.
Young and old together,
We shall not be moved.
Just like a tree that's standing by the water,
We shall not be moved.

Chorus

Black and white together,
We shall not be moved.
Black and white together,
We shall not be moved.
Just like a tree that's standing by the water,
We shall not be moved.

Chorus

We're marching for our children,
We shall not be moved.
We're marching for our parents,
We shall not be moved.
Just like a tree that's standing by the water,
We shall not be moved.

Chorus

Oh, You Can't Get to Heaven

(Please see page 28 for additional lyrics.)

E

Oh, you can't get to heaven on roller skates,

B 7   E   E 7
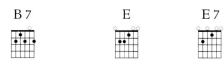

'Cause you'll roll right by those pearly gates.

A

Oh, you can't get to heaven on roller skates,

E

'Cause you'll roll right by those pearly gates.

B 7   E   E 7

I ain't gonna grieve my Lord no more.

A

I ain't gonna grieve my Lord no more,

E

I ain't gonna grieve my Lord no more,

B 7   E

I ain't gonna grieve my Lord no more.

Chorus:

A

I ain't gonna grieve my Lord no more,

E

I ain't gonna grieve my Lord no more,

B 7   E   E 7

I ain't gonna grieve my Lord no more.

A

I ain't gonna grieve my Lord no more,

E

I ain't gonna grieve my Lord no more,

B 7   E

I ain't gonna grieve my Lord no more.

About the Songs

This Little Light of Mine

African-American spirituals (in folk music terminology, "Negro spirituals") like this one originally came to America on ships that carried Africans to be sold as slaves and to live without any rights in horrifying conditions. On the surface, these spirituals were religious songs about the slaves' suffering, which they felt would only end when they went to heaven. But these songs also had a forbidden, secret meaning. They were also prayers for an escape to freedom on the Underground Railroad, a network of inns and homes that sheltered and hid runaway slaves as they headed north to freedom. Spirituals were songs of hope and determination, and that is the way Peter, Paul, & Mary, the trio of which I am a part, sang them during the civil rights movement of the 1960s. We still sing them today, in an effort to create a world of greater freedom, fairness, and peace.

She'll Be Coming 'Round the Mountain

It can be really fun to sing silly songs like this one together. When I was a little boy, I loved to imagine the woman in this song, whoever she was, wearing bright red pajamas, driving a buggy pulled by six white horses, galloping around the corner, and shouting her happy welcome to the whole village that was waiting for her to arrive. Many years later I learned that she may have been "Mother" Jones, a famous union organizer who, in the 1920s, inspired coal miners from the Appalachian mountains to organize for fair pay, better working conditions, and an end to child labor.

Hey, Lolly, Lolly

This song is so enjoyable because everyone gets to make up verses to it as they go along. I made up a bunch for this recording. Can you guess which ones? Actually, it doesn't matter. What matters is that people think of ideas while the first, traditional verses are sung and then come up with new ones that are just as funny. It's a challenge to make up verses on the spot. Try it. Soon you'll get the hang of it, and so will your friends.

Home on the Range

There are some special ways to show your love of your country and "Home on the Range" is a beautiful example. You can really feel the love Dr. Brewster M. Higley had for the western plains of the United States, with their expanses of land almost untouched by civilization, when he wrote these lyrics in the 1870s. The music was added by Daniel E. Kelly and the song was passed from person to person, which was the way people learned songs before radio was in common use. In 1947 Kansas adopted "Home on the Range" as its state song but, unofficially, it is considered the anthem of the American West. Today when I sing it, I think about how important it is to keep the beauty of the western plains from being spoiled.

Blue-Tail Fly

"Blue-Tail Fly" was written more than 150 years ago but, like almost all of the songs in this collection, nobody really knows for sure who wrote it. People who study folk music generally agree that this jolly song is really about a very serious matter: the death of a slave master whose horse, when bitten by a blue-tail fly, rears up and throws his master in a ditch, killing him. The slave is happy his cruel master won't be around to make him miserable anymore, and we wonder if the slave deliberately did not brush away the blue-tail fly. Maybe so! Nobody knows. As for what the words "Jimmy crack corn" mean, your guess is as good as mine. Deciding for yourself what these old songs mean is part of the fun of folk music.

Hey, Ho, Nobody Home

This very old song originally came from England and is called a round, which means that people sing it by starting at different times. At first, singing rounds takes concentration because you have to listen to yourself and also listen to the other parts. Singing rounds is a great way to learn to do what I do when I both sing and play the guitar, and also sing a harmony with someone else. The more you play and sing folk music the more interesting it becomes and the more fun it gets.

My Bonnie Lies over the Ocean

This is a 250-year-old folk song that at first seems to be about the love between a man and a woman, but it's actually about a longing for Prince Charles Edward Stuart, known as Bonnie Prince Charlie, to come back and rule England, where his grandfather once was king. The history behind this song is not as important to me as how this song shows someone feeling sad. Sharing sorrow and grief is important, because when people are lonely and sad they need to know that someone understands and cares about them. Folk songs like this help us to discover an important part of ourselves. They help teach us how to become more loving, more understanding, and more sympathetic toward one another.

John Jacob Jingleheimer Schmidt

What's most special about this song is the way each verse gets softer and softer until the last verse, when everyone sings it at full volume and becomes very silly. Actually, when you sing it together, in the second to last verse just move your lips but don't make a sound at all. That's the one part that I couldn't record. (You had to see me, Bethany, and the children singing to get the joke.)

I'm on My Way

Like the other African-American spirituals in this collection, "I'm on My Way" is partly about slaves being received in the promised land, or heaven, where they believed they would finally be released from the horror of their lives. But this song also allowed slaves to secretly sing of their determination to escape to the north to states where slavery was not permitted. Today, when we sing this song, we rejoice that so much has happened—and continues to happen—since that earlier time to right the terrible wrongs of slavery. The song reminds us that we must always continue to struggle and work toward achieving freedom, justice, and equality for everyone, and respect every person for who they are, regardless of how different they may be from us.

We Shall Not Be Moved

This song is typical of the combination of the two strands of music that make American music so different from the music of other countries. Early American music combined the songs of European countries with African music brought over by slaves. The combination of these two kinds of music produced not only American folk music, but jazz, the blues, country music, and rock and roll. "We Shall Not Be Moved," which has its roots in African-American spirituals, says that we are all one and that we will stand firm in our resolve to act as caring, loving, respectful people to one another. Historically, this song has been a popular union song, sung on the marches for the betterment of the lives of working people.

Down by the Riverside

This famous folk song also originated as an African-American spiritual but became best known during the anti-war movement that blossomed in the 1950s. I have committed my life to speaking out against war and to finding peaceful ways to settle conflicts among nations. Children must grow up learning the habits of peaceful conflict resolution so that they will bring this knowledge to their adult lives. When I sing this song, I always recommit to doing my utmost to find a way to end war. When you sing this song, I hope you will make a similar commitment.

Oh, You Can't Get to Heaven

This delightful song, like "Hey, Lolly, Lolly," also asks us to make up verses as we go along. I ended this book and CD with this fun song because I believe that our task in life is to find creative and joyful solutions when life presents us with problems. If we sing together—when we celebrate, when we mourn, when we are happy, or when we are sad—we will always share the gift of being with friends who understand us, care about us, and accept us just the way we are. Singing together has been a great comfort and joy in my life and I hope it will be in yours, too.

About the Author

Peter Yarrow's career has spanned close to five decades as a member of the legendary folk trio Peter, Paul, & Mary, who became known to many as a voice of their generation's conscience, awakening and inspiring others to help make the world a more just, equitable, and peaceful place. Today, Yarrow devotes the majority of his time to running Operation Respect, a nonprofit he founded in 1999 that received a unanimous vote of Congress honoring its work to create respectful, safe, and bully-free environments for children in schools across America and beyond. Besides numerous awards for his artistry and his public service, Peter has received two honorary doctorates for his steadfast work in the educational arena.

For many years, Peter Yarrow dreamed of recording his favorite folk songs in a very simple, intimate way—the way he first heard them sung as a child. Along with his daughter, Bethany Yarrow, a gifted singer in her own right, Peter shares the songs that first moved and inspired him to become the renowned folk singer he is today. When asked what he would most want to give the generations that follow him, Peter said, "I would give them these songs that helped me come to realize what, for me, is really important in life—people, love, work, and service to each other. I believe that all children can be helped to discover what's important to them in their lives, through these songs. It's magic, in a way, but it seems to happen every time!"

About the Illustrator

Terry Widener's relationship with folk music began as a child in Oklahoma, where he was surrounded by classic folk songs performed by singers like Woody Guthrie. Folk music had made a big impact on the region during the Dustbowl era, and as Terry grew up, this music was an essential part of his heritage.

Inspired by a passion for art, Terry studied graphic design at the University of Tulsa. He has illustrated more than twenty books, including *If the Shoe Fits* by Gary Soto, *Steel Town* by Jonah Winter, and *Lou Gehrig: The Luckiest Man* by David Adler. His picture books have won numerous accolades including a Boston Globe–Horn Book Honor Award, an ALA Notable Children's Book Award, and the California Young Reader Medal.

A father of three, Terry currently resides in McKinney, Texas, with his wife, Leslie.

CD Credits

Produced by Peter Yarrow and Kevin Salem

Peter Yarrow: Lead Vocals, Guitar

Bethany Yarrow: Lead Vocals

Mary Rower: Harmony Vocal on We Shall Not Be Moved;

Paul Prestopino: Banjo, Mandolin, Mandola, Guitars (6 and 12 string), Dobro, Ukulele, Jew's Harp, Harmonica

Dick Kniss: Bass

Recorded, Engineered, Mixed and Mastered by Kevin Salem, Woodstock, New York

Background Vocals:

Maralina Gabriel

Olivia Gabriel

Delilah Dougan

Lucia Legnini

Special Thanks

Marcus Leaver, Frances Gilbert, Robert Agis, Leigh Ann Ambrosi, Paula Allen, Kaylee Davis, Derry Wilkens, Wendy Raffel, Rachel Jackson, Tony Arancio, Beth Bradford, Kate Hyman